Geronimo Stilton
ENGLISH!

11 THE DAYS OF THE WEEK 星期

新雅文化事業有限公司
www.sunya.com.hk

Geronimo Stilton English
THE DAYS OF THE WEEK 星期

作　　者：Geronimo Stilton 謝利連摩・史提頓
譯　　者：申倩
責任編輯：王燕參
封面繪圖：Giuseppe Facciotto
插圖繪畫：Claudio Cernuschi, Andrea Denegri, Daria Cerchi
內文設計：Angela Ficarelli, Raffaella Picozzi
出　　版：新雅文化事業有限公司
　　　　　香港筲箕灣耀興道3號東匯廣場9樓
　　　　　營銷部電話：（852）2562 0161
　　　　　客戶服務部電話：（852）2976 6559
　　　　　傳真：（852）2597 4003
　　　　　網址：http://www.sunya.com.hk
　　　　　電郵：marketing@sunya.com.hk
發　　行：香港聯合書刊物流有限公司
　　　　　香港新界大埔汀麗路36號中華商務印刷大廈3字樓
　　　　　電話：（852）2150 2100　傳真：（852）2407 3062
　　　　　電郵：info@suplogistics.com.hk
印　　刷：C & C Offset Printing Co.,Ltd
　　　　　香港新界大埔汀麗路36號
版　　次：二〇一一年六月初版
　　　　　10 9 8 7 6 5 4 3 2 1

ISBN: 978-962-08-5367-8
© 2007 Edizioni Piemme S.p.A., Via Tiziano 32 - 20145 Milano - Italia
International Rights © 2007 Atlantyca S.p.A. - via Leopardi, 8, Milano - Italy
© 2011 for this Work in Traditional Chinese language, Sun Ya Publications (HK) Ltd.
9/F, Eastern Central Plaza, 3 Yiu Hing Rd, Shau Kei Wan, Hong Kong
Published and printed in Hong Kong

CONTENTS
目 錄

BENJAMIN'S CLASSMATES
班哲文的老師和同學們

Maestra Topitilla
托比蒂拉・德・托比莉斯

Rarin
拉琳

Diego
迪哥

Rupa
露芭

Tui
杜爾

David
大衛

Sakura
櫻花

Mohamed
穆哈麥德

Tian Kai
田凱

Oliver
奧利佛

Milenko
米蘭哥

Trippo
特里普

Carmen
卡敏

Atina
阿提娜

Esmeralda
愛絲梅拉達

Pandora
潘朵拉

Takeshi
北野

Kuti
菊花

Benjamin
班哲文

Hsing
阿星

Laura
羅拉

Kiku
奇哥

Antonia
安東妮婭

Liza
麗莎

GERONIMO AND
HIS FRIENDS
謝利連摩和他的家鼠朋友們

謝利連摩・史提頓 Geronimo Stilton
一個古怪的傢伙，簡直可以說是一隻笨拙的文化鼠。他是
《鼠民公報》的總裁，正花盡心思改變報紙業的歷史。

菲・史提頓 Tea Stilton
謝利連摩的妹妹，她是《鼠民公報》的特派記者，同
時也是一個運動愛好者。

班哲文・史提頓 Benjamin Stilton
謝利連摩的小姪兒，常被叔叔稱作「我的
小乳酪」，是一隻感情豐富的小老鼠。

潘朵拉・華之鼠 Pandora Woz
柏蒂・活力鼠的姨甥女、班哲文最好的朋友，
是一隻活潑開朗的小老鼠。

柏蒂・活力鼠 Patty Spring
美麗迷人的電視新聞工作者，致力於她熱愛的電視事業。

賴皮 Trappola
謝利連摩的表弟，非常喜歡食物，風趣幽默，是一隻饞
嘴、愛開玩笑的老鼠，善於將歡樂傳遞給每一隻鼠。

麗萍姑媽 Zia Lippa
謝利連摩的姑媽，對鼠十分友善，又和藹可親，只想將
最好的給身邊的鼠。

艾拿 Iena
謝利連摩的好朋友，充滿活力，熱愛各項運動，他希望
能把對運動的熱誠傳給謝利連摩。

史奎克・愛管閒事鼠 Ficcanaso Squitt
謝利連摩的好朋友，是一個非常有頭腦的私家
偵探，總是穿着一件黃色的乾濕樓。

EVERY DAY TOGETHER
共度每一天

親愛的小朋友，今天是非比尋常的一天！為什麼呢？為什麼呢？為什麼呢？答案簡單極了，就像吃一份雙倍乳酪的奶昔那樣簡單！你還不明白嗎？好吧，讓我說清楚一點……今天是特別的一天，因為今天我們要學習說……一星期的不同日子！是的，就是一星期的每一天！當然是用英語說啦！不過首先我們要學習怎樣用英語在一天的不同時刻與別人打招呼。請你跟我一起說吧！

跟我謝利連摩・史提頓一起學英文，
就像玩遊戲一樣簡單好玩！

你可以一邊看着圖畫一邊讀。
以下有幾個標誌，你要特別留意：

當看到 💿 標誌時，你可以聽CD，
一邊聽，一邊跟着朗讀，還可以跟
着一起唱歌。

當看到 ★ 標誌時，你可以和朋友
們一起玩遊戲，或者嘗試回答問
題。題目很簡單，它們對鞏固你所
學過的內容很有幫助。

當看到 ❗ 標誌時，你要注意看一
下格子裏的生字，反覆唸幾遍，掌
握發音。

最後，不要忘記完成小測驗和練習
冊裏的問題！看看你有多聰明吧。

祝大家學得開開心心！

謝利連摩・史提頓

GREETINGS 打招呼

同學們想學習在一天不同的時刻怎樣跟別人打招呼，於是托比蒂拉老師詳細地向他們逐一講解。你也一起來學習吧！

You say...

A SONG FOR YOU! Track 1

I Say Goodbye!

The sun is in the sky
and I say good morning,
I meet my friends
and I say goodbye!
I leave the school
and I say good afternoon,
I drink my tea
and I say goodbye!
Good morning, good afternoon,
good evening, good night,
we play together and I say goodbye!
The dinner is ready
and I say good evening,
I eat an apple and I say goodbye!
It's time to go to bed
and I say good night,
I put my pajamas on
and I say goodbye!
Good morning, good afternoon,
good evening, good night,
we play together and I say goodbye!

Good morning

You say good morning from the beginning of the day until twelve o'clock.

Good afternoon

You say good afternoon from twelve o'clock until five p.m.

Good evening

You say good evening from five p.m. until you go to bed.

Good night

You say good night when you go to bed.

TIMETABLE 上課時間表

潘朵拉迫不及待地想學習一星期裏每一天的英文說法，於是她舉起手問托比蒂拉老師能不能馬上教他們怎麼說。剛好托比蒂拉老師拿出一張上課時間表給同學們看，上面除了寫出星期一到星期五的英文名稱外，還有各個學科的英文名稱呢！請你跟着托比蒂拉老師一起說說看。

	Monday	Tuesday	Wednesday	Thursday	Friday
8:30	English	Chinese	Chinese	Mathematics	Chinese
9:30	English	Mathematics	Chinese	Mathematics	English
10:30	Break	Break	Break	Break	Break
10:45	General Studies	General Studies	Art	General Studies	General Studies
11:45	Chinese	English	Art	English	Mathematics
12:45	Lunch	Lunch	Lunch	Lunch	Lunch
14:30	Physical Education	Chinese	Mathematics	Science	English
15:30	Physical Education	Music	English	Science	Music

Children go to school at a quarter past eight in the morning. Lessons start at half past eight.

When lessons are over, at half past four in the afternoon, children go home.

9

THE DAYS OF THE WEEK
星期

托比蒂拉老師講課時，班哲文和潘朵拉一時沒留心聽課，所以沒弄清楚每一天用英語該怎麼說，於是托比蒂拉老師又再給他們講解了一遍。

Sunday
Monday
Tuesday
Wednesday
Thursday
Friday
Saturday

為了考考同學們是不是已經學會了有關星期的英文說法，托比蒂拉老師提出了一些問題，讓同學們接着說下去。一起來看看同學們說得對不對，然後跟着他們一起說說看。

1st	first	第一
2nd	second	第二
3rd	third	第三
4th	fourth	第四
5th	fifth	第五
6th	sixth	第六
7th	seventh	第七

The first day of the week is...Sunday.
The second day of the week is...Monday.
The third day of the week is...Tuesday.
The fourth day of the week is...Wednesday.
The fifth day of the week is...Thursday.
The sixth day of the week is...Friday.
The seventh day of the week is...Saturday.

The fifth day of the week is Thursday.
The third day of the week is Tuesday.
The first day of the week is Sunday.
：案答

10
一星期的第一天用英語該怎麼説？
第三天呢？第五天呢？

ON MONDAY　星期一

同學們已經學會了一星期裏每一天的英文說法，現在托比蒂拉老師要告訴同學們星期一英文課的內容。你也跟着他們一起學習吧。

	Monday
8:30	English
9:30	English
10:30	Break

 I like writing.　我喜歡寫作。

The English lesson starts at half past eight and ends at half past ten.

During the lesson we listen to the teacher, we repeat new words and write them in our exercise books...

... we colour drawings, sing and play together.

I like listening to English words.

I like writing in English.

I like repeating English.

ON TUESDAY 星期二

今天是星期二，同學們正在上數學課，他們碰到很多關於數字和運算的詞彙，你也跟着他們一起學習吧！

Tuesday
Chinese
Mathematics
Break
General Studies

On Tuesday my pupils have mathematics. They learn to do additions and subtractions, multiplications and divisions.

additions 加法
subtractions 減法
multiplications 乘法
divisions 除法

What is two plus three?

Two plus three is five!

2+3 =

What is ten minus four?

Ten minus four is six!

10-4 =

What is three times three?

Three times three is nine!

3x3 =

What is twelve divided by two?

Twelve divided by two is six!

12÷2 =

⭐ 用英語讀出下面的算式，然後計算出答案，並用英語說出來。

1. 2 × 3 =
2. 2 + 9 =
3. 17 − 5 =
4. 24 ÷ 4 =

plus 加
minus 減
times 乘
divided by （被某數）除

答案：
1. Two times three is six.
2. Two plus nine is eleven.
3. Seventeen minus five is twelve.
4. Twenty-four divided by four is six.

12

除了學習計算外，同學們還要學習圖形！班哲文很喜歡學習圖形，但潘朵拉就不那麼喜歡了……請你跟他們一起學習吧！

Sometimes, instead of mathematics, we learn about shapes.

I draw different shapes in my exercise book.

A large and a small square.

A large and a small rectangle.

A large and a small triangle.

A large and a small circle.

⭐ 比較下面各組圖形的大小，然後用英語説出來。（例如：a large triangle）

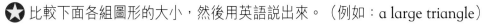

1

2

3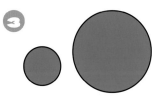

3. a small circle; a large circle
2. a large rectangle; a small rectangle
1. a large triangle; a small triangle
答案：

ON WEDNESDAY 星期三

潘朵拉最喜歡的科目是美術，因為可以塗塗畫畫，還可以用黏土捏出各種造型，真是太好玩了！你也跟着他們一起學習吧！

Wednesday
Chinese
Chinese
Break
Art
Art

I like drawing with crayons.

She likes modelling clay.

He likes painting.

班哲文想給他的圖畫填上顏色，但他有幾種顏色剛好用完了，於是潘朵拉告訴他怎樣用其他顏色混合成那些缺少的顏色。你不相信嗎？一起來看看班哲文是怎樣做得到的，然後跟他一起用英語說說看。

Dip your brush into some yellow and some red.

Yellow and red make orange.

Dip your brush into some blue and some red.

Blue and red make purple.

Dip your brush into some yellow and some blue.

Yellow and blue make green.

YESTERDAY, TODAY, TOMORROW
昨天、今天、明天

上完美術課後，托比蒂拉老師為同學們安排了一個小遊戲。太好了！是猜謎遊戲！你也一起來玩吧！

> **What day is it today?**
> 今天是星期幾？
> **the day before yesterday**
> 前天

Sunday
Monday
Tuesday
Wednesday
Thursday
Friday
Saturday

Yesterday was Sunday and tomorrow is Tuesday.

If today is Thursday, the day before yesterday was...

What day is it today?

It's Monday.

Tuesday!

ON THURSDAY 星期四

星期四有科學課，這是穆哈麥德最喜歡上的課，因為他最愛做實驗，尤其是關於植物和蔬菜的實驗。一起來看看同學們正在做什麼，然後跟他們一起說說看。

On Thursday afternoon, we have science.

During the lesson we observe flowers and plants...

...we plant seeds, water the baby plants, and take care of them.

A few days ago we put some beans on a layer of cotton wool.

Today little plants sprouted from the beans.

Tomorrow we will put the plants into some pots.

ON FRIDAY　星期五

在班哲文就讀的學校裏，每個學生都要選擇一種自己喜歡的樂器學習。所以每逢星期五上音樂課時，課室裏就會馬上變成一個大演奏會！還好托比蒂拉老師知道怎樣協調整個樂隊！

Friday
Chinese
English
Break
General Studies
Mathematics
Lunch
English
Music

在音樂室裏，有以下這些樂器和音樂器材：

triangle 　　**recorder** 　　**cymbals** 　　**drum**

records 　　**CD player** 　　**CD**

I like playing the drum.

We like playing the recorder.

She can play the piano.

He can play the guitar.

 1. 潘朵拉喜歡什麼樂器？班哲文呢？
請用英語回答。

 2. 你會演奏哪種樂器呢？
請用英語回答。

1. Pandora likes playing the drum. Benjamin likes playing the recorder.

答案：

17

ON SUNDAY WE PLAY
星期天，我們會去玩

　　終於到了星期天，這天不用上學，可以盡情地去玩了。班哲文和潘朵拉最喜歡在星期天和我一起玩。這次他們發明了一個遊戲，我以一千塊莫澤雷勒乳酪發誓，這個遊戲真的很好玩。現在請你先跟着他們一起用英語說說遊戲的玩法吧！

How to Play:

1 Write the names of the days of the week on seven cards.

2 On seven other cards, write these actions:

I go to school.
I play tennis.
I play football.
I paint pictures.
I go to the playground.
I meet my friends.
I sleep until ten o'clock.

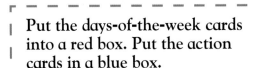

3 Put the days-of-the-week cards into a red box. Put the action cards in a blue box.

4 In turns, pick one card from the red box and one from the blue box.

5 The player who draws cards has to say the day of the week and then mime the sentence.
On Monday... I go to school.

On Monday... I go to school.

! in turns　輪流
draw cards　抽卡

A SONG FOR YOU! Track 2

The Days of the Week

Sunday, Monday, Tuesday, Wednesday, sing now all together!

Thursday, Friday, Saturday, too: these are the days of the week!

6 The first player to say the English sentence correctly gets one point.

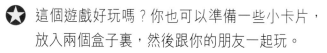
這個遊戲好玩嗎？你也可以準備一些小卡片，放入兩個盒子裏，然後跟你的朋友一起玩。

YOU'RE LATE!

It's Tuesday morning. It's eight o'clock. It's the perfect day for a trip to the seaside.

Tea is in her car. She's picking up Geronimo, Benjamin, Pandora and Trappola. But Trappola's not there.

When are we leaving?

As soon as Trappola gets here!

Where's Trappola?

I don't know. He's late, as usual!

〈你遲到了！〉

星期二早上，八點。今天是最適合到海邊去旅行的好日子。

菲駕着車子來接載謝利連摩、班哲文、潘朵拉和賴皮，但是賴皮還未到。

班哲文：我們什麼時候出發？
菲：等賴皮一到就馬上出發。
潘朵拉：賴皮在哪裏？
謝利連摩：我不知道。他遲到了就像平時一樣。

Fifteen minutes go by, but Trappola doesn't show up.

We were supposed to meet at eight o'clock.

It's a quarter past eight now...

... but Trappola is not here!

I'll call him immediately!

十五分鐘過去了，但是賴皮還沒出現。
菲：我們原本約好八點鐘見面的。
班哲文：現在已經八點十五分了⋯⋯

菲：⋯⋯但賴皮還沒到！
謝利連摩：我立刻打電話給他！

Everybody is waiting, but where is Trappola?

每個人都在等着，但賴皮在哪裏呢？

He's at home, having a gigantic breakfast with ten croissants, and a pear and cheese milkshake.

The telephone rings...

原來他在家裏，正在品嘗一份很巨大的早餐，十個牛角包，一杯梨和乳酪奶昔。
這時，電話響了……

Trappola is startled, he jumps and answers the phone.

Hello, who is speaking?

賴皮嚇了一跳，他從椅子上跳起來去接電話。
賴皮：你好，請問是哪一位？

This is Geronimo. Are you coming?

Coming... where?

謝利連摩：我是謝利連摩。你是不是正在趕來？
賴皮：趕來……去哪兒？

Oh, Trappola! You forgot our trip to the seaside!

謝利連摩：哦，賴皮！你忘記今天約了我們去海邊旅行！

賴皮：什麼旅行？你是說星期四的旅行嗎？

謝利連摩：不，不是星期四！是星期二，賴皮！今天是星期二！

賴皮：哦，對不起！我把星期二寫成了星期四！

賴皮：哦，我真的遲到了！

於是賴皮三步併作兩步衝出屋外，急忙騎上他的單車，向謝利連摩的家駛去。
賴皮：我來了！！！

Trappola pedals as fast as he can, but the traffic lights are red and he has to stop.

賴皮拚盡全力地踩呀踩，卻偏偏遇上紅燈亮着，他只得停下來。

He stops at the zebra crossing to let pedestrians cross the street.

他停在斑馬線前，讓行人先過馬路。

It's half past nine You're late!

At last, Trappola reaches Geronimo's house.

Did you bring your marbles?

Actually, I was in a hurry and I forgot them...

最後，賴皮終於來到謝利連摩的家了。

菲：現在已經九點半了，你遲到了！

班哲文：你有沒有帶彈珠呀？

賴皮：說實話，我太趕了，所以我忘記了帶……

Uncle G has brought them!

Let's go now!

潘朵拉：幸好謝利連摩叔叔帶了彈珠！

菲：我們現在出發吧！

Tell us a joke, Trappola!

Sure! I have a brand-new one ...

He's always late, but he always knows how to make us laugh.

The End

潘朵拉：賴皮，講一個笑話給我們聽吧！

賴皮：沒問題，我有一個全新的笑話……

謝利連摩：雖然他經常遲到，但他每次總是帶給我們很多歡樂！

23

TEST 小測驗

⭐ 1. 你還記得怎樣用英語説一星期裏的每一天嗎？説説看。

⭐ 2. 你知道一星期的第二天和第四天用英語該怎麼説嗎？説説看。

> (a) The second day of the week is ...

> (b) The fourth day of the week is ...

⭐ 3. 用英語讀出下面的算式，然後計算出答案，並用英語説出來。（例如：Two plus three is five.）

> (a) $2 \times 4 =$ (b) $5 + 9 =$ (c) $12 - 5 =$ (d) $14 \div 2 =$

⭐ 4. 比較下面各組圖形的大小，然後用英語説出來。（例如：a large circle）

(a)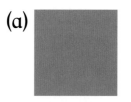

(b)

⭐ 5. 下面圖畫中的小朋友在做什麼？如果圖畫下面的句子是正確的，就説 True；如果是不正確的，就説 False。

(a)

He likes modelling clay.

(b)

She likes drawing with crayons.

(c)

He likes painting.

⭐ 6. 用英語説出以下樂器的名稱。

(a)   (b)   (c)   (d)

DICTIONARY 詞典

（英、粵、普發聲）

A

action 動作

additions 加法

art 美術

as usual 像平時一樣

B

beans 豆

beginning 開始

bike 單車

brand-new 全新的

break 小息

breakfast 早餐

bring 帶

brush 畫筆

C

cheese 乳酪

Chinese 中文

circle 圓形

clay 黏土

correctly 正確地

cotton wool 棉花

crayons 蠟筆

croissants 牛角包

cymbals 鈸

D

different 不同的

dinner 晚餐

divided by （被某數）除

divisions 除法

draw cards 抽卡

drink 喝

drum 鼓

E

ends 結束

English 英文

guitar 結他（普：吉他）

F

fifth 第五

first 第一

football 足球

forgot 忘記

fourth 第四

Friday 星期五

I

if 假如

immediately 立刻

in turns 輪流

J

joke 笑話

G

general studies 常識

gigantic 巨大的

go by 過去了

go home 回家

good afternoon 午安

good evening

　晚上好（傍晚時分）

good morning 早安

good night

　晚安（睡覺之前）

greetings 打招呼

L

late 遲到

laugh 笑

leave 離開

lessons 課堂

listen 聽

lunch 午餐

M

mathematics 數學

meet 遇見

milkshake 奶昔

minus 減

Monday 星期一

multiplications 乘法

music 音樂

O

observe 觀察

other 其他

P

pedestrians 行人

physical education 體育

piano 鋼琴

plants 植物

playground 遊樂場

plus 加

pots 花盆

pupils 學生

purple 紫色

pajamas 睡衣

R

ready 準備好

really 真的

recorder 牧童笛

records 唱片

rectangle 長方形

repeat 重複

S

Saturday 星期六

science 科學

seaside 海邊

second 第二

seeds 種子

sentence 句子

seventh 第七

shapes 形狀

show up 出現

sixth 第六

sometimes 有時

sorry 對不起

sprouted 發芽

square　正方形

subtractions　減法

Sunday　星期天

T

take care　照顧

telephone　電話

tennis　網球

third　第三

Thursday　星期四

times　乘

timetable　時間表

today　今天

tomorrow　明天

traffic lights　交通燈

triangle　三角形 / 三角鐵

trip　旅行

Tuesday　星期二

U

until　直至

W

waiting　等着

water　澆水

Wednesday　星期三

week　星期

words　字

Y

yesterday　昨天

Z

zebra crossing　斑馬線

看在一千塊莫澤雷勒乳酪的份上，你學得開心嗎？很開心，對不對？好極了！跟你一起跳舞唱歌我也很開心！我等着你下次繼續跟班哲文和潘朵拉一起玩一起學英語呀。現在要說再見了，當然是用英語說啦！

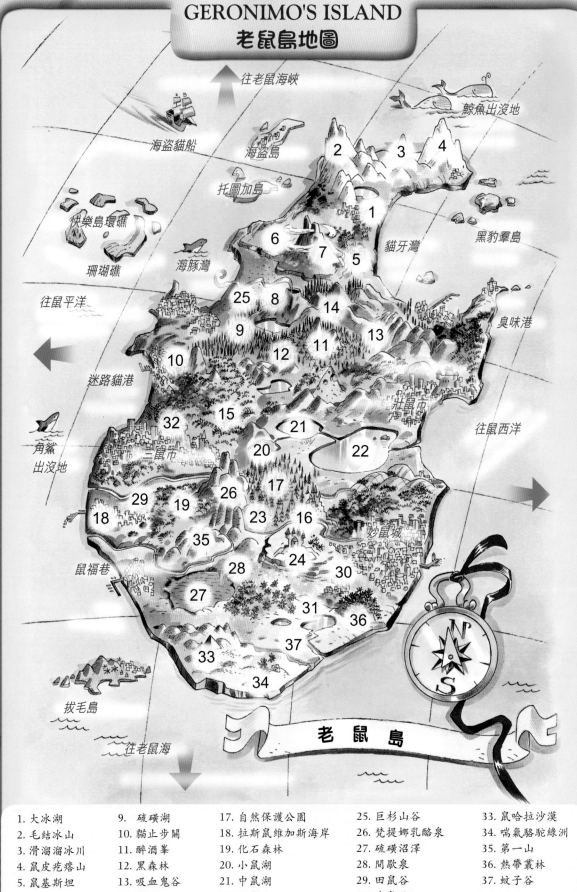

GERONIMO'S ISLAND
老鼠島地圖

老鼠島

1. 大冰湖	9. 硫磺湖	17. 自然保護公園	25. 巨杉山谷	33. 鼠哈拉沙漠
2. 毛結冰山	10. 貓止步關	18. 拉斯鼠維加斯海岸	26. 梵提娜乳酪泉	34. 喘氣駱駝綠洲
3. 滑溜溜冰川	11. 醉酒峯	19. 化石森林	27. 硫磺沼澤	35. 第一山
4. 鼠皮疙瘩山	12. 黑森林	20. 小鼠湖	28. 間歇泉	36. 熱帶叢林
5. 鼠基斯坦	13. 吸血鬼谷	21. 中鼠湖	29. 田鼠谷	37. 蚊子谷
6. 鼠坦尼亞	14. 發冷山	22. 大鼠湖	30. 瘋鼠谷	
7. 吸血鬼山	15. 黑影關	23. 諾比奧拉乳酪峯	31. 蚊子沼澤	
8. 鐵板鼠火山	16. 吝嗇鼠城堡	24. 肯尼貓城堡	32. 史卓奇諾乳酪城堡	

Geronimo Stilton

EXERCISE BOOK

練習冊

想知道自己對 THE DAYS OF THE WEEK 掌握了多少，
趕快打開後面的練習完成它吧！

ENGLISH!

11 THE DAYS OF THE WEEK　星期

THE DAYS OF THE WEEK
星期

⭐ 小朋友，你知道一星期裏的每一天用英語怎麼説嗎？在橫線上寫出來，然後給圖畫填上顏色。

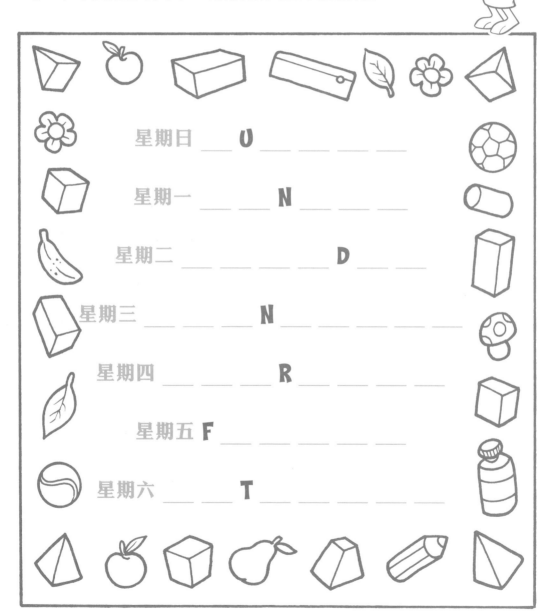

星期日 __ __ U __ __ __ __

星期一 __ __ __ N __ __ __

星期二 __ __ __ __ __ D __ __

星期三 __ __ __ __ N __ __ __ __

星期四 __ __ __ __ R __ __ __ __

星期五 F __ __ __ __ __

星期六 __ __ T __ __ __ __ __

BENJAMIN'S TIMETABLE
班哲文的上課時間表

★ 根據班哲文的上課時間表，圈出正確的答案。（可圈多於一個答案）

	Monday	Tuesday	Wednesday	Thursday	Friday
8:30	English	Chinese	Chinese	Mathematics	Chinese
9:30	English	Mathematics	Chinese	Mathematics	English
10:30	Break	Break	Break	Break	Break
10:45	General Studies	General Studies	Art	General Studies	General Studies
11:45	Chinese	English	Art	English	Mathematics
12:45	Lunch	Lunch	Lunch	Lunch	Lunch
14:30	Physical Education	Chinese	Mathematics	Science	English
15:30	Physical Education	Music	English	Science	Music

1. What lessons does Benjamin have on Monday?

Mathematics　　　　English　　　　Science

Physical Education

2. Which day does Benjamin have music?

Tuesday　　　Wednesday　　　Thursday　　　Friday

AN ENGLISH LESSON
上英文課

⭐ 同學們上英文課時會做些什麼？從下面選出適當的詞彙，填在橫線上，完成句子。

drawings	English	words	write

1.

I listen to _____ words.

2.

I _____ in English.

3.

I repeat English _____ .

4.

I colour _____ .

3

A MATHEMATICS LESSON
上數學課

⭐ 1. 根據托比蒂拉老師提出的數學問題，在橫線上寫出答案。
（先寫阿拉伯數字，再寫出英文數字）

(a)

What is ten plus three?

10 + 3 = _____   Ten plus three is _____ .

(b)

What is twenty minus four?

20 − 4 = _____   Twenty minus four is _____ .

(c)

What is five times five?

5 × 5 = _____   Five times five is _____ .

(d)

What is fourteen divided by two?

14 ÷ 2 = _____   Fourteen divided by two is_____ .

 2. 根據指示，給正確的圖形填上顏色。

(a)
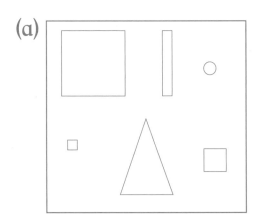

Colour the large square.

(b)
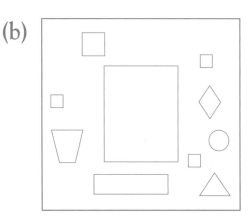

Colour three small squares which have the same size.

(c)
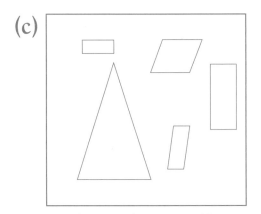

Colour the small rectangle.

(d)
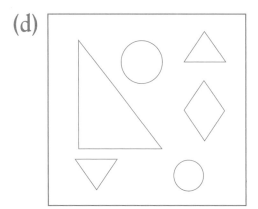

Colour a triangle.

(e)
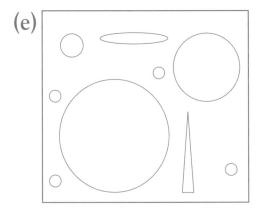

Colour four small circles which have the same size.

(f)
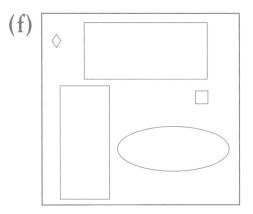

Colour a rectangle.

I LIKE PAINTING
我喜歡畫畫

★ 當兩種顏色重疊時，猜一猜會產生一種什麼新顏色呢？根據提示，在橫線上填寫適當的詞彙，然後把橢圓形填上相應的顏色。

提示： orange　　　　purple　　　　green

1.

yellow　　　　　　　red

Yellow and red mixed together make _____ .

2.

yellow　　　　　　　blue

Yellow and blue mixed together make _____ .

3.

blue　　　　　　　red

Blue and red mixed together make _____ .

6

A SCIENCE LESSON
上科學課

⭐ 從下面選出適當的詞彙填在橫線上，完成句子。

beans

plants

cotton

pots

science

1. A few days ago they put some _____ on a layer of _____ wool.

2. Today little _____ sprouted from the beans.

3. Tomorrow they will put the plants into some _____ .

ANSWERS 答案

TEST 小測驗

1. Sunday   Monday   Tuesday   Wednesday   Thursday   Friday   Saturday
2. (a) The second day of the week is <u>Monday.</u>   (b) The fourth day of the week is <u>Wednesday.</u>
3. (a) Two times four is eight.   (b) Five plus nine is fourteen.
   (c) Twelve minus five is seven.   (d) Fourteen divided by two is seven.
4. (a) a large square; a small square   (b) a large circle; a small circle
5. (a) False   (b) False   (c) True
6. (a) triangle   (b) recorder   (c) cymbals   (d) drum

EXERCISE BOOK 練習冊

P.1

S U N D A Y   M O N D A Y   T U E S D A Y   W E D N E S D A Y
T H U R S D A Y   F R I D A Y   S A T U R D A Y

P.2

1. English, Physical Education   2. Tuesday, Friday

P.3

1. English   2. write   3. words   4. drawings

P.4-5

1. (a) 13, thirteen   (b) 16, sixteen   (c) 25, twenty-five   (d) 7, seven
2. (a) (b) (c) (d) (e) (f)

（任選一個
三角形均可）

（任選一個長
方形均可）

P.6

1. orange   2. green   3. purple   1-3 填色：略

P.7

1. beans, cotton   2. plants   3. pots